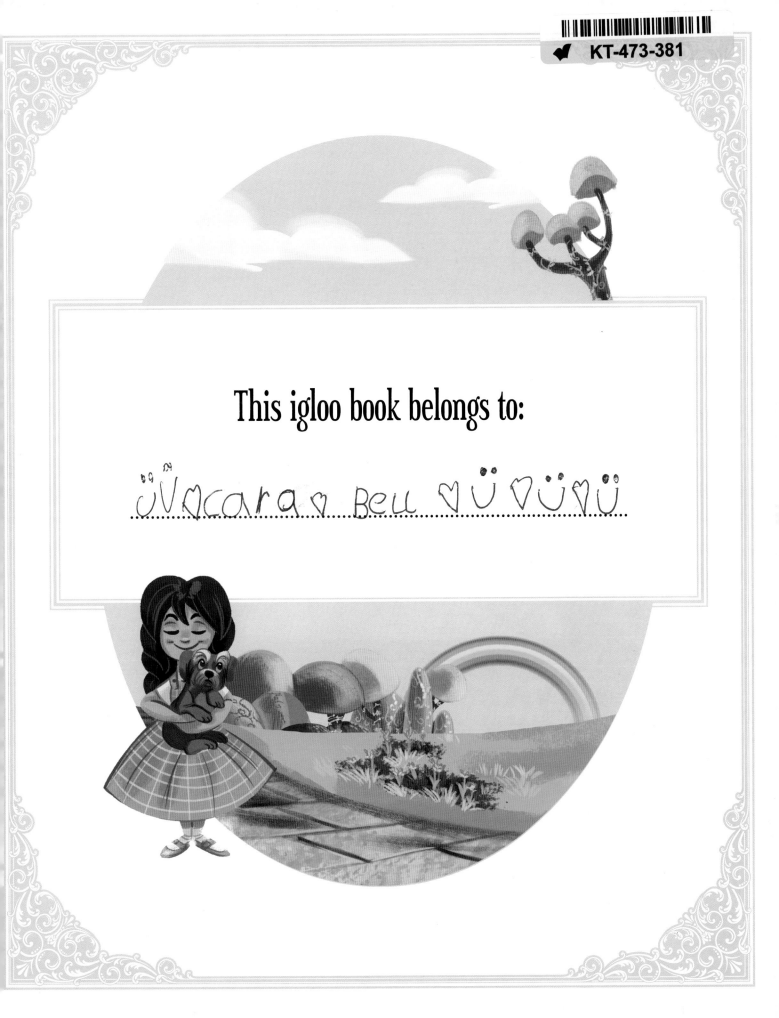

This igloo book belongs to:

Ñacara Bell

igloobooks

Published in 2021
First published in the UK by Igloo Books Ltd
An imprint of Igloo Books Ltd
Cottage Farm, NN6 0BJ, UK
Owned by Bonnier Books
Sveavägen 56, Stockholm, Sweden
www.igloobooks.com

0221 004
8 10 12 11 9 7
ISBN 978-1-78557-927-1

Based on the original story by L. Frank Baum
Illustrated by Jacqui Davis
Written by Melanie Joyce

Cover designed by Lee Italiano
Interiors designed by Justine Ablett
and Katie Messenger
Edited by Hannah Cather

Printed and manufactured in China

The Wizard of Oz

igloobooks

Once, on the great Kansas prairies, a girl called Dorothy lived with her Uncle Henry, who was a farmer, Aunt Em, who was his wife, and a little dog called Toto. All around the farmhouse where they lived, as far as the eye could see, was flat, dry, sun-baked earth.

One day, a fierce wind came swirling from the North. "Cyclone!" cried Uncle Henry, running to get the cows from the field.

Dorothy grabbed Toto and dashed inside, but the little house shook and the terrible wind lifted it up as if it were as light as a feather.

The wind **wailed** and the house **swayed**. Hour after hour passed
and Dorothy grew so tired that she lay down and fell asleep.

Then, suddenly, the house landed with a
THUD!

Jumping up, Dorothy flung open the door.
Outside wasn't the dry prairie,
but a beautiful land of tall,
colourful trees, sparkling streams
and pretty flowers.

Out of the trees came a group of small people.
"Welcome to the land of the Munchkins," said a lady with
a kind face. **"I am the Witch of the North. You have saved
us from the Wicked Witch of the East."**

Dorothy's house had fallen on a witch! All that remained was a pair of silver shoes.

"Oh, dear!" cried Dorothy. "I want to go home to Kansas."

"The Wizard of Oz will help you," said the Witch of the North. "Wear these shoes and follow the yellow brick road to the Emerald City. There, you will find the wizard."

Dorothy put on the silver shoes and started on her journey.
"Come along, Toto," she said.

They had not gone far when they came upon a scarecrow in a field of golden corn.

"Good day," said the scarecrow.
"Where are you going?"

"To see the great Wizard of Oz," replied Dorothy.
"Can he give me a brain?" asked the scarecrow, for he had a head full of straw.
"I am sure he would," replied Dorothy and they set off together.

Soon they came to a forest, where they found a man made of tin. He was so rusty he could not move.

"This oil will do the trick," said Dorothy, pouring it on the tin man's joints. She told him all about the journey to Oz.

"I want to come, too," he said. "I want the Wizard of Oz to give me a heart!"

So, Dorothy, Scarecrow and Tin Man set off into the forest.

Suddenly, there was a
ROAR!
as a lion bounded
out of the trees.

Toto barked and the lion opened his mouth as if to bite him.
"Don't you dare bite poor little Toto!" cried
Dorothy, slapping the lion on his nose. **"You're just a big coward."**

The lion hung his head in shame.
"I know I am," he said. "I guess I was just
born this way. I wish I had courage."

"The Wizard of Oz will give you courage," said Dorothy,
who felt sorry for the cowardly lion. "You can come with us."

The friends travelled on and at last they came to the gates of the **dazzling** Emerald City. Everything was green. The houses were green and even the people, too. The Guardian of the Gates led them through the streets until they came to the palace of the great wizard.

Dorothy was taken to the throne room, but all she found was a giant stone head.

"I am Oz! Why do you seek me?" boomed the head.

Dorothy explained that she wanted to go home to Kansas, that Scarecrow wanted a brain, Tin Man, a heart and Lion, courage.

"I shall grant these wishes, if you kill the Wicked Witch of the West," said the voice. Dorothy did not want to kill the witch, but knew that she must.

The Wicked Witch of the West could see great distances.
She saw Dorothy and her friends approaching, so she
sent crows and winged monkeys to capture them.

Scarecrow and Tin Man fought
them off, but Dorothy and Lion
were captured. The witch made
Dorothy her servant, but what she
really wanted was Dorothy's shoes,
for she knew they had great power.

After many days, Dorothy became so angry
that she **threw** water over the witch.

"What have you done?"
screamed the witch, angrily.
"Now I shall melt awaaaay!"

The witch melted and disappeared altogether.
Dorothy quickly freed Lion and, with Scarecrow
and Tin Man, returned at once to the wizard's palace.

When the group reached the palace's throne room, they heard a loud voice, **"Who are you and why do you seek me?"**

"Where are you?" asked Dorothy. **"We cannot see anyone!"**

ROAR! went the Lion, scaring Toto, who knocked over a screen.

Behind it was a small, grey-haired old man.

"I am the wizard," said the old man, sheepishly, his voice trembling. "I will do anything you ask."

"Keep your promises!" cried Dorothy, sternly.

The wizard gave Scarecrow a brain, Tin Man a heart and Lion, courage. However, he did not have the power to send Dorothy back to Kansas.

"We can go in a balloon," said the wizard.
"That is how I came to Oz."

Just as it was about to take off, Toto ran away,
so Dorothy chased after him. **"Hurry!"** cried
the wizard, but the balloon floated away. The balloon
rose further into the sky and that was the last
anyone saw of the wonderful Wizard of Oz.

"Now I'll never get back to Kansas!" sobbed Dorothy.

"Glinda, the Witch of the South, may help," said Scarecrow. **"The road to her castle is dangerous, but she is your only hope of getting home, Dorothy."**

So, once again, the friends set off...

... through **enchanted** forests...

... where the trees seemed to come alive and **fierce** creatures lurked.

At last, they reached Glinda's castle.

"How can I help you, my child?"
asked the beautiful witch.

"My greatest
wish is to get
back to Kansas,"
said Dorothy.

Glinda smiled. "Just knock the heels of your shoes
together three times and say where you wish to go."